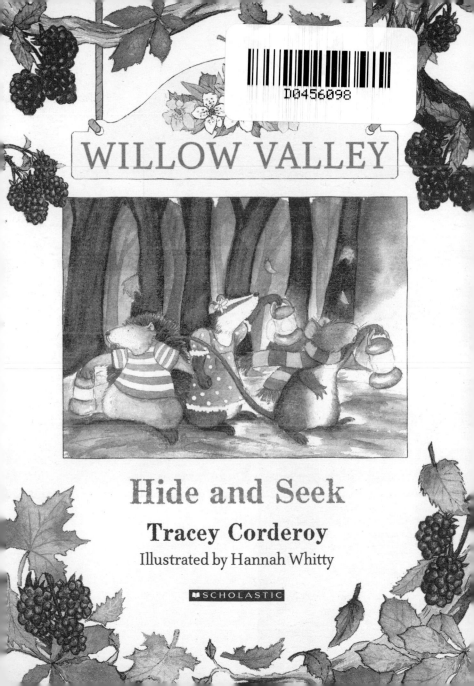

WILLOW VALLEY

Hide and Seek

Tracey Corderoy

Illustrated by Hannah Whitty

SCHOLASTIC

First published in the UK in 2012 by Scholastic Children's Books
An imprint of Scholastic Ltd
Euston House, 24 Eversholt Street
London, NW1 1DB, UK
Registered office: Westfield Road, Southam, Warwickshire, CV47 0RA
SCHOLASTIC and associated logos are trademarks and/
or registered trademarks of Scholastic Inc.

ISBN 978 1 407 12477 3

A CIP catalogue record for this book
is available from the British Library.

Printed and bound by CPI Group (UK) Ltd, Croydon, CR0 4YY
Papers used by Scholastic Children's Books
are made from wood grown in sustainable forests.

1 3 5 7 9 10 8 6 4 2

This is a work of fiction. Names, characters, places, incidents
and dialogues are products of the author's imagination or are used
fictitiously. Any resemblance to actual people, living or dead,
events or locales is entirely coincidental.

www.scholastic.co.uk/zone
www.traceycorderoy.com

For Jenny and the children of

Leighterton Primary School. . .

T.C. x

WILLOW VALLEY

STUMPY'S STYLE

POPPY FIELD

BUTTON-OAK MILL

PODRICK HARE'S HOUSE

TEN OAKS FIELD

ALLOTMENTS

BUTTERCUP MEADOW

MOSSY HOLLOW

HORATIO'S HOUSE

WILLOUGHBY WHITE-WHISKERS' HOUSE

ACORNS SCHOOL

LIBRARY

BLUEBELL WOOD

VILLAGE SQUARE

STARLA'S HOUSE

BAKERS

TOY SHOP

HOOT HILL BARN

MUMFORD MOLE'S HOUSE

THE DARK WOOD

MARTHA RABBIT'S HOUSE

OLD CROOKED STONE BRIDGE

RILEY'S HOUSE

Chapter 1

It was a cold, crisp morning in Willow Valley. The rushes by the river's edge were dusted with sparkling frost and spiders sat in icy webs, as stony-still as statues.

Riley stood on the riverbank wrapped in his stripey scarf and wearing some warm red mittens his mum had made.

He gazed out at three narrowboats that were bobbing about on the river, his little white whiskers rippling with excitement.

Each of the boats gleamed and twinkled in the watery morning sunlight. They'd been cleaned from top to bottom and looked like new!

At the front was the *Kingfisher*. This was the captain's boat, and it was the colour of a summer sky. Behind it sat the *Whirligig*, which was the biggest boat and dark blue in colour, with little beetles and pale pink roses painted around its windows.

The *Dragonfly* was at the back. This

was bottle green in colour with a bright red door and was decorated with lacy-winged dragonflies.

The animals of Willow Valley were about to set off on a market trip. Every family would go and the trips were so much fun! They would sail the boats out of the valley into the open countryside,

stopping here and there to sell their home-made goods.

This was to be the last trip before Christmas and Riley couldn't wait! Very soon they'd be sailing down to Dingle Creek. Riley remembered it from last year. It had a wood with giant fir trees, a pretty stream with stepping-stones and a *huge* meadow, just right for playing hide-and-seek!

When the animals of Willow Valley got there, they'd set up their market on the riverbank just beside the wood. Then the Dingle Creek animals would hurry down to buy their home-made treats.

Riley loved helping serve on the stalls. It was so much fun! *"Eeek!"* he squeaked excitedly. It was nearly time to go!

He watched as a team of badgers loaded the *Dragonfly* with the goods to be sold. There were baskets of freshly baked pasties and crumbles. There were warm woolly scarves and mittens. There were big jars of pickles and wreaths of bright holly to hang on front doors at Christmas time. Riley hoped there would be one left over for *his* little cave-house!

For weeks now everyone had been

cooking and knitting, getting everything
ready for today. Even Riley had helped
pick the last of the apples
for the crumbles.

For him the trips meant lots of fun
too – playing explorers or mean old
pirates and sleeping on wobbly
bunk beds!

Even though families went together,
the children all got to sleep in the same
room. Riley thought it made the trip even
more of an adventure – like the best
kind of sleepover, with all his friends!

There were sometimes even secret
midnight feasts. Riley and his friends

loved these. They'd huddle by torchlight under Riley's quilt, nibbling biscuits and hoping that no one would hear them!

Suddenly, Riley heard the sound of footsteps. He spun around to see his two best friends, Starla and Horatio, racing down the hill. They should have been here ten minutes ago! Riley had wanted to board the boats before anyone else. Most likely Horatio had wanted *three* breakfasts again!

"Riley!" shouted Starla. The little badger waved and a big furry smile spread across her face.

"Hi!" cried Riley, waving back.

"Ugh!" groaned Horatio Spark, the roly-poly hedgehog thumping along beside Starla. He waved and gave a big sticky smile, spraying cake crumbs everywhere.

It looked like it was ginger cake.

Horatio *loved* ginger cake – even more than tightrope walking or trying to pole vault to the moon!

Horatio, in fact, loved *many* things – most of which got him into trouble! He never meant any harm, though. He just liked to *do* things, that was all. . .

"Phew!" panted Starla, racing up. "I'm so excited about the trip! Sorry we're late. Horatio was, um . . . *hungry!*"

"*Ery* ungy!" Horatio muttered, his mouth so full that his cheeks puffed out and he looked like a prickly hamster! He swallowed and licked his lips. Then he heaved up a heavy picnic basket.

"Guess what *I've* brought for the trip?" he beamed.

"Err . . . ginger cake?" giggled Starla.

"How did you guess?" gasped Horatio. "I've got some gingerbread men too! One each for you two and two each for me!"

"Hey, that's not fair!" grinned Riley, making a leap for the basket.

"No, wait!" cried Starla, pointing a paw. "Look!"

All over the hills, cave-house doors were opening and animals were pattering out. There were badgers and rabbits, moles and mice, squirrels and voles and hedgehogs!

They wore bright scarves and mittens, and on their backs were rucksacks packed for the trip. Their small eyes twinkled and their ears were pricked up as they hurried to the boats, chattering.

Then Riley spotted his mum and little sister coming along the riverbank. Mimi-Rose was wearing a bunny suit and had a sparkly tiara on her head. *"Riley!"* she squeaked, bouncing over and giving him a hug.

"Mimi-Rose," whispered Riley, as Horatio sniggered, "no hugs in front of my *friends*."

"But I'm a *princess-bunny*!" his sister

giggled. "And princess-bunnies hug a lot!" She tightened her grip and, try as he might, Riley couldn't prise her off.

Lately, Mimi-Rose had been hugging him too much and wanting him to play with her all the time. Always the

same game too – princess-bunnies . . .
princess-bunnies . . . *princess-bunnies*!

"Hey, let *go*," Riley puffed. "Please,
Mimi-Rose – *let go*!"

Finally, he wriggled free. "Riley, be
nice," said his mum. Riley grunted and
shuffled closer to Starla and Horatio.

"We should get to our boat," said Starla,
"or all the best bunks will be gone."

"Yeah," gasped Riley. And the three
friends dashed off, leaving Mimi-Rose
pouting.

"But *I* want to share a bunk bed with
Riley!" she grumbled.

Riley, Starla and Horatio were all

travelling on the *Kingfisher*. Last time
they'd been on the *Whirligig*. Very
few of the animals ever travelled on
the *Dragonfly*, as this was the boat that
carried all the goods to market.

Riley didn't mind though. The
Kingfisher was his favourite boat. Starla's
grandfather, Willoughby White-Whiskers,
sailed it. He was the captain of the fleet
and Riley's hero.

The three friends joined a queue of
other animals walking up the gangplank.
On deck were lots of other families
eager to set sail. Riley looked around
to see which children would be their

shipmates this time.

First he spotted Digby Mole, then Posy Vole and Phoebe Badger. Then he saw Bramble Bunny bounce by with Abigail Bright, a chatty red squirrel. There were *lots* of little brothers and sisters there too. Their boat was going to be crowded!

Suddenly, Abigail grabbed Posy's paw and whisked her off down the deck.

"Horatio, look!" gasped Riley. "They're going to steal *our* bunk!" He and Horatio had bagsied the bunk by the window just last week.

"No *way*," scowled Horatio. "STOP!"

he called, but they didn't even look back.

"Right then," nodded Riley. *"After them!"*

They raced away, the icy air stinging Riley's ears. "Hey!" cried Starla. "Wait for me!" Though she didn't mind which bunk *she* got, as long as it had a big, warm patchwork quilt.

By the time they all reached the bedroom, Abigail and Posy had made themselves comfy on the *best* bunk by the window.

Abigail was sitting on the top bed, her big bushy tail held high, while Posy knelt on the bottom bed, looking smug.

"B-but that's *our* bunk!" Horatio spluttered.

"We got it first," grinned Abigail.

"But we'd *bagsied* it!" Riley cried, stamping his foot hard.

"Too bad!" replied the girls, both giggling.

The argument went on as crowds of little animals scurried into the room, all diving on to bunks and shouting, "Mine!"

Soon there were only two beds left – one on the bottom of Starla's bunk and the one below Mimi-Rose. "Riley!" called his little sister. "This is *our* bunk – *look*!"

Riley plodded over and she beamed at

him. "But I want to share with Horatio," he groaned. "Please will you move and share with Starla? Then Horatio can share with me."

"But *I* want to share with *you*!" said Mimi-Rose.

Riley asked her again . . . and again . . . and *again*, but each time his little sister said, "*Noooo!*"

He'd almost given up when a sudden grin spread across her face. "OK," said Mimi-Rose. "I *will* move!"

"You will?" asked Riley. "Really?"

"Yes!" his sister nodded. "If you *promise* you'll play with me, lots and lots!"

"Hmmm. . ." said Riley. "OK – I promise. But not *all* the time!" he added. Riley had wanted to play with his friends on this trip.

Suddenly, the boat gave a tiny jolt. "I think we're moving!" Starla said.

"Whoa!" cried Riley. "Hey – let's go and see!"

Everyone raced to Abigail's bunk and peered out of her window, their tiny pink noses pressed against the glass as they watched the riverbank glide by.

As Riley gazed out, his warm breath fogged up the freshly cleaned window.

"Yippee!" he squeaked, excitedly. They were off!

Chapter 2

"Time for a game!" Riley cried, scurrying into the middle of the room. "How about pirates?"

"*Hooray!*" cheered everyone. They gathered around Riley.

"But *I* want to play *princess-bunnies*," moaned Mimi-Rose.

Ignoring her, Riley started the game in his best pirate voice. "I'm Captain Black-Paw!" he exclaimed. "And I'm going to find me some *treasure*!"

"I'm Captain Starfish!" Starla giggled.

"And I'm Captain Prickleface!" laughed Horatio.

Abigail's paw suddenly shot in the air. "Oooh, can I be a *shark*?" she said.

"Yes! You'll be great!" Horatio nodded. "Do you want to be a shark too, Mimi-Rose?"

"No, sharks are horrid!" scowled Mimi-Rose. "I'm being a pirate, like Riley!"

The game began. The floor was the ocean and the little ones were deadly sea slugs. An old sock filled with chocolate coins had been buried under the sand. This sand was really Horatio's quilt, which was yellow.

All three captains had to race to it, not touching the ocean or they died! If you died you had to become a shell. "And not even *breathe*!" said Horatio.

They had to watch out for killer seaweed too, which was *really* Abigail's little brother, Bruce, and her best friend, Posy.

There was also the shark with big snappy jaws, which Abigail was especially excited to be, as she had made herself a fin-costume out of a pillowcase.

"Right!" said Riley. "Now for me!" He tied his woolly scarf around his head, over one eye, as if it were an eye patch.

"OK, pirate captains – ready, steady, *GO!*"

At this, all three captains leapt from bed to bed over the deadly ocean. "I feel *seasick*," groaned Bruce the killer seaweed as he rolled around the floor.

"Are you OK, Bruce?" Abigail asked. "Maybe don't sway so much."

She turned round to snap her jaws again when suddenly she noticed Riley. "*Hey*," she gasped. "*Look at Captain Black-Paw!*"

Captain Prickleface spun around. "Shiver me timbers!" he gaped. Riley was already halfway across the ocean and he didn't even look puffed out!

At this rate he was going to get *all* the chocolate treasure!

"Captain Black-Paw's the *best*!" roared Riley. "No one leaps oceans like me!"

He shook his fist at the killer seaweed. He poked out his tongue at the shark. Even the suckers on the deadly sea slugs couldn't zap Captain Black-Paw!

"Aha!" squeaked Riley as he reached the sand where the treasure-sock was buried. He glanced around from Horatio's top bunk, then gave a huge grin.

Captain Starfish was busily fighting off the shark and Captain Prickleface had been grabbed by killer seaweed!

Posy and Bruce were now tickling
his feet. "Hee hee!" laughed Horatio.
"*Geroff!*"

Riley rubbed his paws together, a twinkle in his eye. Then he dived under the sand and started to tunnel for the treasure.

It was as black as night under Horatio's quilt. Riley quickly crawled past Horatio's whiffy bed socks but he couldn't find the treasure-sock anywhere.

When he reached the edge of the sand he poked out his head and looked around. Riley gasped. He wasn't alone up there. Somebody *else* had already got the treasure. . .

"Mimi-Rose!" cried Riley. "Give it back!"

"Mine!" giggled Mimi-Rose.

Riley looked at the sand. It was scattered with wrappers. His sister had been scoffing the treasure! The last chocolate coin was now in her paw, unwrapped and ready to join the rest in her tummy.

"Hand it over!" Riley cried, but Mimi-Rose crammed it into her mouth. As she did, the other two pirate captains appeared.

"Mutiny!" Horatio roared, gaping at the empty foil wrappers.

"Mimi-Rose!" tutted Starla. "What have you done? We were going to *share* that chocolate."

"Yeah!" snapped Riley.

"Huh?" said Horatio. "We *were*?"

"S-sorry," sniffed Mimi-Rose, her face now plastered in chocolate. She hung her head and her bottom lip started to quiver.

"Perhaps we should play something

else?" sighed Starla.

"Yeah," Riley muttered.

"Might as well. . ." said Horatio glumly.

They got off the bed and then everyone played tag. But Mimi-Rose didn't want to play. She kept on tugging Riley's tail and asking him, over and over again, to play princess-bunnies with her.

"You *promised* you'd play with me, Riley!" she squeaked.

"Not *that* game!" whispered Riley.

"But I *love* playing princess-bunnies," she sniffed. "Really, really much!"

Her nagging went on until lunchtime. Then all three boats were tied to the bank and everyone ate lunch on the *Dragonfly*.

As he pattered into the dining room, Riley sniffed the air. He'd recognize that smell anywhere – jacket potatoes with hot melted cheese! "Mmm," he nodded, licking his lips. "Yummy!"

They all had some lettuce and tomatoes too, and chunks of crusty bread. Riley and his friends ate and ate. It felt just like a party!

After lunch, the children went to school on the *Whirligig* as the boats set off down the river once again. They needed to reach Dingle Creek before night, as their market was due to be held there first thing the next morning.

Riley asked their teacher if they could make pirate swords, but Mumford Mole shook his head. "We've got lots of sums to finish!" he said.

"Oh. . ." groaned everyone, their whiskers drooping.

"Maybe tomorrow!" smiled Mr Mole.

"If you're good and helpful at the market!"

"Oooh!" cried everyone excitedly. "We *will* be!"

Supper that night was magical. The *Dragonfly's* long dining room was lit with flickering lanterns and delicious smells wafted through the air.

The friends feasted on pasties that melted in their mouths, and hot buttered carrots and parsnips. Before long everyone's tummy was full, even Horatio's!

As they walked back to the *Kingfisher*, the sky was sprinkled with twinkling stars and the moon shone as bright as a diamond.

Back in the bedroom, Riley snuggled under his quilt, listening to the soft, low lullaby of the river as it lapped the sides of the boat.

Soon his heavy eyes began to close and before he knew it, he was fast asleep. . .

Chapter 3

"Riley, Riley!" squeaked Mimi-Rose, shaking him awake. Riley rubbed his eyes and gave a fluffy stretch. "Market time!" cried his little sister.

She clambered off Riley's bed as he sat up and peered around the room. It was lit with a warm peachy glow as the sun peeped in through the window. Riley sniffed the air. It was going to be a frosty day.

In the beds all around, tiny noses

twitched and paws rubbed sleepy eyes
as, one by one, the animals yawned
awake.

Suddenly, the door creaked open and
Riley's mum came in. "Anyone ready for
breakfast?" she asked, her chocolate-brown
fur thick and shiny.

"Me!" cried a roomful of happy little voices. "I'm ready!"

Everyone scrambled out of bed, their whiskers quivering in the chilly air as they raced to the door like a big, fluffy whirlwind.

"Whoa!" chuckled Riley's mum. "Steady!"

When they were neatly lined up, she led them off the *Kingfisher* and along the bank to the *Dragonfly*'s cosy dining room.

They hurried inside to find everyone from the *Whirligig* tucking into breakfast, along with all the grown-ups from the *Kingfisher*.

Willoughby White-Whiskers, Riley noticed, had nearly finished his porridge. "Morning, Grandpa!" Starla called, waving to him as Riley and Horatio sat down at the long oak table.

"Good morning, Starla!" Willoughby called back. "What a lovely day for the market. I'm just off to start setting up. See you later!"

He got to his feet, patted his tummy, then strolled out of the door as Starla sat down with her friends at the table.

"Hey," said Riley, "let's eat up quickly, and then *we* can go and help out too!"

"OK," Starla nodded.

"Err – yeah!" said Horatio. "As long as I can have seconds!"

Martha Rabbit pattered over with bowls of porridge on a big wooden tray. She popped three down on the table in front of the friends and everyone thanked her.

They blew on their porridge, mixed in some honey, then quickly gobbled it down. When Horatio had finished his second bowl, Riley said, "Come on, let's go!"

He led his friends out of the dining room and down a long, narrow corridor. At the end of it was a bright red door which they opened and hurried through.

They raced up some steps on to the deck, where a chilly breeze suddenly hit them. "Brrr," cried Horatio, rolling into a ball. "I'm f-f-freezing!"

Riley and Starla tickled his feet and

Horatio uncurled with loud giggles.
Then they shivered down the gangplank
and on to the frozen grass.

Although it felt bitterly cold, the sky
was powder blue and Dingle Creek
looked very beautiful.

The sun lit the frosty webs on the
hedgerows, making them glimmer
and shine. And big fluffy robins
sat in the treetops, singing.

The narrowboats were tied to the
riverbank near a little stream. This was
the creek that gave the place its name.

On one side of the creek was a
meadow. On the other side was a wood.

Tiny stepping-stones in the stream's shallow water linked one side to the other, making it very easy to nip back and forth.

Riley really liked it here, though the big open meadow looked odd to him. He was used to the hills in Willow Valley and here it felt like something was missing. A little bit like a room without any walls!

The wood here looked different too. The trees were very tall and pointy – mostly firs and pines and spruces. Big fir cones sat heavily on their branches, whose long, thin leaves looked as sharp as needles.

They reminded Riley of the Christmas tree in Willow Valley's village square, but they weren't like the ones that grew on the rolling hillsides. *Those* trees had big, soft leaves in the summer which shaded Riley from the sun, and in the autumn breeze they rustled, making tinkly music.

Suddenly, Riley spotted Mr White-Whiskers coming down the *Whirligig*'s gangplank. He was carrying a table off the boat with old Podrick Hare. They placed it down beside some others already on the grass and Riley and his friends hurried over.

"Hi, Grandpa!" said Starla. "We've

come to help!"

"Jolly good!" smiled Willoughby White-Whiskers.

"Yep!" Horatio nodded. "We'll do *anything*!"

"Err," said Willoughby, suddenly remembering when Horatio had helped before. Five baskets of pasties and a table had ended up in the river!

Willoughby thought. "Oh, I know!" he said. He fished around in a box on the grass and pulled out a stack of white tablecloths. "Our tables – or should I say *market stalls* now – will need to be covered with these."

"OK!" said Starla brightly. "Leave it to us!"

She took the tablecloths and skipped to the tables. Horatio and Riley followed.

"Hey Riley," said Horatio in a cheeky little whisper. "Watch this!"

He raced up to Starla, swiped a tablecloth and threw it over his head. *"Whooo!"* he moaned. "I am a ghost and I'm coming to get you!"

Horatio bumbled this way and that, unable to see a thing. "*Whooo!*" he giggled, picking up speed and whirling round and round.

"Horatio!" squeaked Riley. "Watch out!"

THUNK!

Horatio crashed into a tree trunk and pulled off the tablecloth crossly.

"What a silly place to put a tree!" he muttered.

"Let's just cover the tables," said Starla. "Come on!"

They got on with the job and soon the

tables were all nicely covered. Suddenly
everyone seemed to be outside, carrying
baskets of goods off the *Dragonfly* and
unloading them on to the stalls.

Three stalls were laid out with plates
of pasties and two with apple crumbles.
Another two were covered with stripey
scarves and mittens.

Three more stalls were stacked high
with cakes – nut loaves and fruitcakes
with gleaming white icing, so sparkly it
looked like snow!

Horatio longed to take a sneaky nibble
and try everything but Starla and Riley
knew him too well and watched him

very closely. No one would want to buy a cake that had a bite taken out of it!

There were also stalls selling jars of pickles and holly wreaths dotted with berries. Jugs of winter crocuses made the stalls look extra pretty, and colourful bunting was draped around the trees.

Finally, Podrick and Mumford Mole hung up a banner saying **Willow Valley Market** and everyone made their way to the stalls they'd be helping on.

"I'm with Grandpa selling cakes!" smiled Starla.

"Pah!" frowned Horatio. "Why can't *I* sell cakes? I've got to sell silly holly wreaths!"

"At least you'll be used to the prickles!" giggled Riley.

Riley and his mum would be selling scarves and mittens. He and his friends hurried to their stalls.

No sooner had they got there when a pattering noise echoed in the air all around. The Dingle Creek folk were on their way to the market!

Then suddenly from the wood and meadow came lots of little animals. In their paws they clutched big, bulging purses and baskets ready to be filled.

"Ho ho!" chuckled Willoughby. "What a crowd today!"

Willow Valley
Market

The next few hours passed in a whirl. The animals of Dingle Creek had never seen so many tempting treats. . .

"Three apple crumbles!" called a fluffy-faced badger.

"Four holly wreaths, please!" cried a hedgehog.

"Eight nut loves!" beamed a tufty-tailed squirrel. "Oh, and I'll take that jug of crocuses too!"

"But those aren't for sale!" giggled Starla.

"Well, make that an *extra* nut loaf instead, then!" smiled the squirrel.

Riley sold lots of scarves too. One mole

and his wife bought *five*! One for each
of them and one each for their three
little ones.

"Matilda, Max, Maisie," said their
father, "say thank you to the mouse."

"Thank you!" giggled the tiny moles,
wrapping their long
scarves round and round
their necks.

When there was nothing left to buy, the animals of Dingle Creek strolled away with full baskets and big smiles on their faces.

"Right!" beamed Willoughby as the last customer left. "Time for lunch! Well done, everyone."

"Hurrah!" cried Horatio. "I'm *starving*!"

Chapter 4

Everyone tidied up before lunch. "Mr White-Whiskers," Riley said, as he and his friends folded tablecloths, "are we having a market tomorrow?"

"Why, yes!" smiled Willoughby. "Just one more! We're stopping off at Otterly Marsh on the way back home."

"But Grandpa," said Starla, "there's nothing left to sell."

"We've got plenty more on the boat!" said Willoughby, winking.

When everything was neatly packed away, they ate lunch on board the *Dragonfly*. It felt so good being back in the warm again.

During the market, Martha had been busy making spicy parsnip soup – just what they needed after a chilly morning on the riverbank.

The dining room smelled delicious as they all sat down. "Everyone tuck in, then!" Willoughby called.

They picked up their spoons and started to eat. The soup was hot and tasty. "Mmm," said Horatio, "after ginger cake, soup is my *favourite*, you know!"

"But you say that about *everything*!" laughed Riley.

Next, they had freshly baked bread and cheese. Riley loved *all* kinds of cheese – even the stinky blue stuff.

"Poo!" grinned Horatio, holding his nose as Riley nibbled on a big chunk. "Actually, that cheese smells a bit like my *bed socks*!"

"No!" snorted Starla. "Your bed socks are *way* smellier!"

After lunch, it was time for school. Mumford Mole led the children across to the *Whirligig* and settled them down in the schoolroom.

A big bright fire roared in the woodburner, making the room all cosy. Suddenly everyone felt like an afternoon nap!

Mr Mole told them to open their desks and they yawned as they took out their books. First they had to write a story about the market. Then they did lots of sums.

When everyone had finished, Riley put up his paw. "Please, Mr Mole," he said politely, "can we make swords now?"

"Err. . ." replied his teacher, looking puzzled.

"You did say we could!" Horatio
nodded. "Yesterday you said if we were
helpful at the market we could make
pirate swords today! And I sold *every
single holly wreath.*"

"And I sold scarves!" cried Riley.

"And I sold lots of cakes!" Starla
nodded. Then everyone else began to
call out the jobs *they* did too.

"I sold . . . fifteen crumbles!" said
Abigail, counting on her fingers
and toes.

"I swept up!" said little Bruce Bright.

"I sold pickles!" Posy beamed.

"And I," said Digby in a shy
little whisper, "did something very
helpful too!"

"We helped him!" boomed Bramble
and Phoebe.

"All right! All right!" chuckled
Mumford Mole. "As you all helped,

we *will* make swords. But only *pretend* ones!" he added.

"Thanks, Mr Mole!" cried everyone. "Yippee!"

They raced to the cupboard and pulled out the craft box. Then they all started cutting and glittering and gluing!

"*My* sword," said Riley, "is going to be huge! As long as the Milky Way!"

"And mine as long as the *universe*!" giggled Starla.

"Well, mine," boasted Horatio, puffing out his chest, "is going to be the longest of all! Yeah – mine's going to be . . . as long as . . . *a really long snake*!"

Soon everyone was clutching a bendy card sword. Now they couldn't *wait* to start playing!

"Ooo arrghh!" cried Starla, in her Captain Starfish voice. "You be a fluffy stowaway!"

"I'm no stowaway!" Riley growled back in *his* pretend pirate voice. "This is the bad ship Black-Paw, ooo arrghh! Off my ship, stripey scoundrel!"

He was about to make Starla walk the plank when Mimi-Rose tugged his tail. "I want to play *princess-bunnies*!" she groaned. "Not pirates *again*!"

"Be gone!" Riley roared, swishing his sword.

"Sword-fight time!" boomed Horatio. Suddenly, their teacher blew his whistle. "Err, how about we go outside?" he said. "You can play pirates out there."

"*Hooray!*" cheered everyone, thundering out, their eyes now wide with excitement. "Yo ho ho!" they sang. "A pirate's life for me!"

Mumford pattered after them. "W-wait – no running on deck!" he called. "And *do* be careful going down that gangplank! Oh dear!"

When they were all in the meadow, Abigail thought it would be really good fun to play pirate hide-and-seek. Everybody else agreed at once, except for Mimi-Rose.

"*But I want to play princess-bunnies!*"
she yelled, glowering at Riley. And she
turned and plodded off through the
icy grass.

Riley sighed as he watched her
go. Maybe he should play *her* game.
He had promised to play with her,
after all. . .

He was just about to go after her when Horatio cried, "Quick! Abigail's already started counting!"

"Let's hide in that hollow tree trunk!" whispered Starla. "Come on!"

Horatio grabbed Riley's paw and whisked him over to a hollow tree trunk lying on the grass. "B-but," stuttered Riley, "my sister's upse—"

"Quick, get in!" Horatio whispered, bundling him inside. He and Starla crawled in behind. Then, with their pirate swords in their paws, they waited.

They could hear lots of footsteps thumping past as everyone raced to hide. "I bet no one finds a place like *this*!" giggled Starla.

Just then, Abigail's voice called out, "Ready or not, here I come!"

"*Eeek!*" squeaked Horatio, jiggling about and almost *bursting* with excitement. "Ooohhh!" he suddenly blurted out. "Everyone keep quiet!"

Riley shot a paw to Horatio's lips as they heard Abigail hurry by. "Now, where *is* everyone?" she muttered to herself.

She seemed to be heading away from them because her footsteps got quieter and quieter. Then suddenly they heard her cry, "Ha!"

"I think she's found someone," Riley nodded. So everyone peeped out to see.

"It's Posy!" whispered Starla. She'd been hiding behind a bush. Now Abigail had a little helper.

They set off together, arm in arm. Riley and his friends watched them go. They saw them skip around the meadow, searching high and low. "They'll never find us!" Horatio whispered. "Never!"

Then suddenly Abigail found Bramble Bunny, who was pretending to be a rock. "But Bramble," she chuckled, "rocks don't have fluffy tails!"

Next, she spotted Digby Mole high up

in a tree. He was tangled in a big ball of
mistletoe and looked very sorry for himself.

"Hey, don't worry!" cried Abigail.
"I'm coming up!"

She shot up the tree trunk, untangled him, and then brought him down on her back.

"What were you doing you up there?" asked Abigail.

"Up where?" whispered Digby, squinting around. His spectacles had slipped off somewhere and he was very short-sighted without them. "But I thought I was tangled up in some *grass*," he blushed.

The next to be spotted was Phoebe Badger. Or rather, her stripey legs were! They were poking out of a hole in the bank and kicking about wildly. She must have got stuck wriggling in to hide.

Everyone grabbed a leg and tugged until – *pop!* – out she came! Then the game of pirate hide-and-seek went on. . .

Finally, there were only *three* pirates left to find – Captain Black-Paw, Captain Prickleface and Captain Starfish. "Riley!" called Abigail. "Horatio! Starla! Watch out, I'm coming to find you!"

Riley and his friends held in giant gasps as Abigail came closer and closer. Suddenly, Horatio couldn't bear it any longer. This game was just *too* exciting! "We're not in the tree trunk!" he blurted out. "Uh oh!"

With that, two bright eyes peeped in.

"Found you!" giggled Abigail.

"Ooo arrghh!" chuckled the three little pirate captains.

They crawled out clutching their swords and the huge group of children waiting outside gave a great big cheer.

"So what shall we play *next*?" Horatio asked.

"How about a walking-the-plank game?" said Riley. "Our tree trunk would make a brilliant plank! And we could . . . we could—"

But Riley stopped and peered around the crowd. "Wait!" he gasped, his eyes growing wide. *"Where's my sister?"*

Chapter 5

Everyone gasped. Mimi-Rose wasn't there.

"She's probably still hiding," said Horatio.

"But she *isn't*!" cried Riley, suddenly remembering. "When I wouldn't play what she wanted, she just wandered off!" If *only* he had followed her. If only. . .

"Don't worry," said Starla. "She's probably not far, but we'd better tell Mr Mole."

"Yeah, OK. . ." sighed Riley, hanging his head.

While the others searched for
Mimi-Rose, Riley, Horatio and Starla
hurried over to their teacher, who was
sitting on the riverbank marking books.
"Enjoying your game?" Mumford
asked. Then he saw their worried faces.

"Oh, whatever's the matter?" he cried, his spectacles slipping down his nose.

"W-we can't f-find my sister," stuttered Riley.

"*What?*" Mumford Mole leapt to his feet. "But how long has she been missing?"

"Since just before we played hide-and-seek," said Riley.

"Um!" gulped their teacher. "Goodness! Don't panic! Best go and get some grown-ups and then we'll search for her all together!"

Riley nodded gloomily.

"It'll be OK," Starla said.

"Yeah," Horatio nodded.

Mumford blew on his whistle and the children in the meadow suddenly looked across. "Children, come over here!" he said.

The class hurried over and as Mumford led them on to the *Dragonfly*, the sun slipped behind a cloud. Riley sniffed the air. It was going to be another cold night and very soon it would start getting dark.

On board the *Dragonfly*, most of the grown-ups were checking the goods for the Otterly Marsh market.

"Mum!" cried Riley, running to her. "We can't find Mimi-Rose! I saw her before and then . . . then I didn't. And now *nobody's*

seen her! And I think . . . I think – it was
all m-my fault b-because—"

Riley stopped to take a breath, but
before he could say another word,

Willoughby put a paw on his shoulder. "Steady, my boy," said the old badger softly.

Willoughby now looked at Riley's mum. "Don't worry," he said with a little nod. "We'll find her."

He and Podrick quickly handed out some lanterns and everyone trooped off the boat. The sky was now a steely grey and Dingle Creek looked gloomy as everyone began to search for Mimi-Rose.

The squirrels checked up all the trees, while the voles, mice, badgers and hedgehogs searched the low bushes on the ground.

The moles checked the hollowed-out tree trunks by crawling right the way through them. Their eyesight might be bad but no one could tunnel like *them*!

As Riley searched, he thought about his sister. The very last time he'd seen her she was stomping off in her bunny suit. Then suddenly he remembered something. . .

"Princess-bunnies!" gasped Riley.

What if she'd gone to find some *real* princess-bunnies? There had been bunnies at the market earlier, Riley was sure of it! Could that be where Mimi-Rose had gone?

He raced over to Starla and Horatio, who were busy searching a blackberry bush. "Hey!" he puffed. "I think my sister's gone into Dingle Wood! She's been wanting to play princess-bunnies all day and I bet she's gone off to try and *find* some!"

"Huh?" said Horatio.

"Really?" gasped Starla.

"She was heading back to where the market had been the last time I saw her!" said Riley.

He thought for a moment. Dingle Wood was *just* across the creek. "I'm going to have a quick look," he said.

"I'll come too!" Starla nodded.

"OK, and me," said Horatio. "B-but just to the edge. . ."

Clutching their lanterns, they crossed over the creek using the trail of stepping-stones.

Then Riley led them into the wood between two giant fir trees. "Come on!" he called behind him. "This way!"

They stopped by some toadstools, raised their lanterns and peered around for a glimpse of white fur.

"I wish I'd brought my umbrella," Horatio sighed, gazing up into the trees.

"It's not going to rain just yet," said Riley, sniffing the air again.

"I know," said Horatio. "But look at those fir cones – they're as big as cannon balls! If those rain down on us, they'll squash us flat!"

They carried on searching until

suddenly Starla spotted something on the ground. She padded over and picked it up. "Oooh," she gasped. "Look!"

It was a shiny pink jewel, shaped like a heart. Riley knew it at once. "It's off my sister's princess tiara!" he said.

He took it out of Starla's paw and held it up to his lantern. "So we were right. She did come into the wood!"

Riley felt his heart begin to thump. All around him were tall fir trees. The wood was getting thicker the further they went in. What if they couldn't *find* Mimi-Rose?

"Sh-shall we go and fetch Mr White-Whiskers?" he asked.

"Yep, good thinking!" said Horatio.

"Wait!" cried Starla. *"What's that noise?"*

Chapter 6

Rustle, rustle!

There it was again! But what could be making the sound? "M-Mimi-Rose," murmured Riley, "i-is that you?"

Then suddenly someone giggled from behind an old tree stump. As it wasn't a scary giggle, Riley and his friends went to look.

Three tiny moles were huddled behind the stump, all of them giggling madly. Riley knew them at once from the scarves they were wearing, wrapped round and round their necks. They were the moles he'd served at the market – Matilda, Max and Maisie.

"Hoghedge!" giggled little Max, squinting up at Horatio.

"Badder!" chuckled his two little sisters. "Hee hee!"

Riley didn't know why they were laughing so much, but *something* had given them the giggles.

At that moment, a door in a mossy mound opened and their father poked out his head. "Tea-time, children!" he called. "Hot crumpets today!"

He was just about to go back inside
when he spotted Riley and his friends.
"Oh!" he said, squinting hard. "You're
the little mouse from the market!"

Riley pattered over clutching his
lantern as the sky above the trees grew
darker. "I'm looking for my little sister,"
he said. "Have you seen her?"

The mole wriggled out of the mossy mound, his red front door still wide open. Riley could see his wife inside, buttering hot crumpets at the table. Then the dreamy smell wafted under his nose.

"Your sister?" said Daddy Mole. "She'd be a little mouse too, then?"

"A snowy white one," Starla nodded. "She was helping at our market too."

"Princess-bunny!" giggled Maisie. Then her brother and sister laughed too. They rolled around on the chilly ground, chuckling and chuckling.

"Have you spotted my sister?" asked Riley. The sight of Mimi-Rose in her very odd outfit might *well* have given them the giggles.

"Lots of princess-bunnies!" Matilda chuckled.

"More bunnies?" said Starla. "Riley, you were right – she *did* go looking for bunnies!"

"So where do they live?" Horatio asked.

"Why, just through that clump of trees there!" said Daddy Mole, pointing. "If you could just hold on a moment, I'll show you!"

He scooped up his giggly babies and popped them inside for their crumpets. Then he led the way to the clump of trees. "Just over here," he nodded. "Follow me!"

As they got closer, Riley heard happy voices. "A cup of tea for me!" laughed one.

"A cream bun for me!" said another.

"Yes, your majesties!" giggled a third, and Riley knew *that* voice.

"It's Mimi-Rose!" he cried. "I think we've found her!"

They raced to the trees. Just beyond was a clearing which had been made to look like a café. Tree stumps had been covered with gingham cloths and rocks were now pretend chairs.

"This is my café!" beamed Mimi-Rose, suddenly spotting her brother. "The princess-bunnies have come to my café and I'm making them their tea. There'll be lots of washing up to do!" she giggled.

Riley didn't know what to say. His sister had found some ordinary bunnies and had dressed them up like *princesses*! They had crowns of ivy on their heads and wore leafy gowns and little cloaks woven out of grass.

In their paws were tiny acorn-shell teacups and pretend cakes made out of fir cones. Mimi-Rose had a funny twig pencil in her paw and was writing

down their orders in a notebook she'd
made from some old scraps of bark. It
looked like she was having a *lovely* time.

"Mimi-*Rose*," frowned Riley. "I was
worried about you! You shouldn't have
wandered off!"

"But you wouldn't *play* with me," said
his little sister.

She looked at Riley with big, dark
eyes. It was true – he hadn't *really*
played with her, though he had promised
that he would. And promises shouldn't
be broken. . .

"Here," said Riley, holding out her
jewel. "I'm sorry I didn't play with you."

She took it from him. "I'm sorry I wandered off too!"

Suddenly, they heard loud footsteps. *"Mimi-Rose!"* called their mum, dashing through the trees with Willoughby at her side. "Oh, *there* you are! *Thank goodness we've found you!"*

She threw her arms around both her children. "Mum," blushed Riley, "*I* didn't get lost!"

"I know! I know!" panted Riley's mum, planting big kisses on their heads. Riley felt the tips of his ears turn pink. Then his mum looked at Mimi-Rose.

"You must never wander off again!"

she said in quite a stern voice.

"I won't," murmured Mimi-Rose. "I *promise*!"

The tiny white mouse beamed up at her mum, then took her brother's paw. And *this* time Riley didn't wriggle free.

"I don't suppose," Horatio muttered, "your princess café sells *real* cakes?"

"Oh Horatio!" giggled everyone.

"What?" grinned Horatio. "I'm *starving*."

Willoughby nodded. "Right, then!" he said. "If I'm not mistaken, it's about to get very dark!"

And sure enough, as they gazed up, they saw a big silvery moon through the trees. "Time we got back to the boats then, I think!" said Willoughby.

They waved goodbye to the princess-bunnies (who were now sweeping up the café!) and left Daddy Mole at his little red front door.

Back on the *Kingfisher* it was warm and cosy. Soon it would be suppertime – toad-in-the-hole tonight!

"Do they use *real* toads?" Horatio asked as they trooped past the dining room.

"No! Don't be silly!" giggled Starla.

They went to the bedroom to wait for supper. Everyone was there and all the children were so happy to see Mimi-Rose.

They crowded around her and she drew them a picture of her princess-bunny café. "And I made all the cakes *myself*!" she said proudly.

Horatio then settled down on the rug to polish his pirate sword, whilst Starla curled up in a chair with her fairy-tale book.

This just left Riley, who sat on his bed
thinking about the day. He was glad
that he'd been the one to find his sister.

Mimi-Rose could be a bit annoying
sometimes, but she was the only
sister he had and he wouldn't want
her any other way.

"Um, Mimi-Rose," he called to her. "I'll play princess-bunnies tomorrow if you like?"

"And me!" cried Starla.

"And me!" grinned Horatio.

"Us too!" called everyone.

Tomorrow was going to be a great day. They had another market stop at Otterly Marsh, and then it was back to Willow Valley – the *best* place in the whole world. . .

Look out for more

WILLOW VALLEY

titles – out now!

WILLOW VALLEY

Birthday Fun
Tracey Corderoy

"I wish I lived in Willow Valley!" Philippa Forrester

WILLOW

Spooky Sleepover
Tracey Corderoy

"I wish I lived in Willow Valley!" Philippa Forrester

LOW VALLEY

The Big Bike Race
Tracey Corderoy

"I wish I lived in Willow Valley!" Philippa Forrester